Victorian Tales

Terror on the Train

This second edition first published 2016 by
Bloomsbury Education, an imprint of Bloomsbury Publishing Plc
50 Bedford Square, London, WC1B 3DP

www.bloomsbury.com

First published in 2012 by A & C Black Limited.

Bloomsbury is a registered trademark of Bloomsbury Publishing Plc

Text copyright © Terry Deary 2012, 2016
Illustrations © Helen Flook 2012

A CIP catalogue for this book is available from the British Library

ISBN: 978 1 4729 3937 1 (paperback)

Printed and Bound by CPI Group (UK) Ltd, Croydon CR0 4YY

1 3 5 7 9 10 8 6 4 2

TERRY DEARY

Victorian Tales

Terror on the Train

Inside illustrations by
Helen Flook

BLOOMSBURY EDUCATION
AN IMPRINT OF BLOOMSBURY

LONDON OXFORD NEW YORK NEW DELHI SYDNEY

Chapter 1

Staplehurst, Kent, England, 9 June 1865

"B-b-b-b-b..." little Tommy Bucket stuttered.

The boy turned his round eyes to look down the railway track. His eyes were wild and afraid. "B-b-b-b-b..." he tried again. The more afraid he was, the more the words tripped over his terrified tongue.

Old John Benge placed a hard-skinned hand on each of the boy's shoulders. "Tommy..."

"B-b-b-b-b..."

"Quiet, Tommy. We have a job to do."

The man spoke as if he were talking to a simple-minded child. But Tommy was bright behind the wide eyes and the button nose. He just struggled to speak, ever since his first day on the South Eastern Railway.

The memory of that first day still came to him every evening in nightmares.

The accident. The moment when Old John Benge cried, "Look out Tommy!"

The boy had turned to see a coal truck rolling towards him. He was standing in the middle of the track and his boots seemed stuck to the sleepers. The truck creaked and groaned, rolled and rattled and loomed larger than the summer sky over him.

Tommy had stretched out a hand as if he could stop the towering truck in its tracks. His heel caught on a wooden block and he fell backwards. It saved his life. He fell between the iron rails as the wagon rolled above him. He wanted to close his eyes and scream. His eyes were stuck open and his throat too tight to let out a squeak.

When the gang of track-layers reached him they hauled him to his feet. He was as stiff as one of their iron rails and twice as cold.

"We shouted stand clear," Michael Leary moaned.

"The boy has a touch of deafness," Old John, their foreman, sighed. "Never mind. He's still alive, that's all that matters."

But little Tommy took a week to stop shaking, and suddenly started to stutter when he grew excited. A month after his accident, he still trembled at the sight of the tracks. But his mother needed the money he brought home. So he swallowed his fears and his tears and went to work with the railway men.

He didn't say much, and he didn't hear everything, but he understood. And now he just *had* to remind Old John in any way he could.

"B-b-b-b-b..."

"It's safe, young Tommy. Trust me."

Tommy put his lips together and blew them out. "*Poosh*!" He made his fingers explode outwards at the same time.

The old man smiled and showed his pink-grey gums. "Bang? B-b-b...bang? Is that what you are trying to say?"

He wrapped an arm around Tommy's shoulder and they walked by the side of the track where the summer corn in the fields was waving gold and green. "Clever boy," Old John said.

Tommy frowned. "The w-warning," he said.

"Quite right," Old John said. "We are pulling up the rails over the Staplehurst bridge to put down new ones. We need to know if a train is going to come along and fall in the river."

Tommy nodded.

"So we should set a banger on the track a mile away. If we hear a bang then we know a train is coming. Clever boy. Did your dad teach you that?"

The boy nodded again.

The old foreman reached inside his pocket and pulled out a book.

"I have something better than a banger, Tommy lad. I have a railway timetable. See?"

He jabbed a ragged and dirty fingernail at the page.

"A train at twelve noon, and no more trains till four o'clock in the afternoon. We have four hours after the ten o'clock train goes through."

The man pulled a fat silver watch from the pocket of his waistcoat. He turned an ear towards the distant hills.

"And if I am not mistaken – and I am *never* mistaken – then that is the twelve o'clock express train on its way."

Tommy turned and saw the grey feather of smoke growing larger as the train drew closer. The rails beneath his feet began to tremble and he stepped onto the gravel path at the side of the track.

The train driver saw them, gave a screech of the steam-whistle, and the metal monster was on them in a few seconds. First the engine, then the carriages roared past them like an earthquake. Tommy's teeth seemed to shake in his head. It was scary and exciting.

Old John Benge put his watch in his pocket. "Dead on time," he said. "Now, let's get that old track ripped up."

It was two minutes past twelve.

Chapter 2

Thirty miles away in Folkestone, the station clock showed thirty-five minutes past two. The mighty express engine hissed and steamed like the breath of an ice giant.

Matilda Mudding held tight to the hand of the man beside her. "Ooh, Mr Dickens. It looks like it's going to explode."

Charles Dickens sighed. "This is the South-east Railway's best engine. It will not explode."

"Promise?"

"I promise. Now climb aboard. Miss Ternan is waiting for you. A good maid is always ready when her mistress calls," the man said, and shook his head so his long mane of hair scattered the steam.

"Yes, Mr Dickens, sir, yes, sir," the girl jabbered and pulled herself up into the carriage.

The great writer Charles Dickens looked up at the cab of the engine.

"What time will we reach London?" he asked the driver.

"Twenty-five minutes after four, Mr Dickens, all being well," the driver said, wiping sweat from his brow with a dirty handkerchief.

Dickens nodded. "In time for tea. Good man," he said and turned to follow the maid.

"Oh, Mr Dickens?" the driver called. "I love your latest story, *Our Mutual Friend*. I read the new part every month."

"Thank you," the writer said and gave a small bow of the head.

"So tell me, how does it end?" the driver asked.

Dickens smiled and patted the brown leather case he was carrying.

"It's a secret... and it's all here in my case. Drive carefully. We don't want any harm to come to it, do we?"

"Lor' no," the driver laughed. "I'd die if I didn't find out. That Silas Wegg with his wooden leg ... funniest thing I read in years."

The writer smiled and climbed on board the train. The train guard waved a flag and blew his whistle. Steam hissed and mighty wheels screamed as they skidded over the rails, then took hold and started to haul the eight coaches out of the station.

3:05 p.m.

Matilda wanted to look out of the window at the flying fields and the rolling hills but Miss Ternan and her mother kept her too

busy. With "comb my hair" and "find my
book" and "pass me my sickness tablets"
and "where is my sewing?" and "pour me
a glass of water", Matilda was running
between the two women.

Charles Dickens sat in a corner and
smiled gently. He took a fountain pen

from his pocket and began to write in a notebook. Matilda was breathless but managed to ask, "Are you writing *Our Mutual Friend*, Mr Dickens, sir?"

The man looked up and smiled.

"The chapter I am writing now is about Miss Bella Wilfer on her wedding day. Each month they will print a new part," he told her and patted the leather case beside him. "This one will appear in August. It is the sixteenth part," he said quietly.

"Is it a tale of a poor orphan boy like Oliver Twist? I loved that book, Mr Dickens. It's the best book in the world," Matilda sighed.

"This is not quite the same. It's a tale of a girl, Bella, who was born into a poor family," the writer said.

"Like me," Matilda nodded.

Before Dickens could answer, Ellen Ternan snapped, "Find me a hatpin, girl. This rattling train is shaking my hat off my head."

As Matilda rummaged in the lady's travelling case she asked, "How fast are we going, Mr Dickens, sir?"

"Forty miles an hour or more," he said looking out of the window at trees gliding past.

"And where are we?"

The writer put down his pen and squinted ahead. "The middle of Kent... we're not far from Staplehurst Station," he said.

"Will we stop?"

"No, we won't be stopping at Staplehurst," Dickens told the serving girl.

But Charles Dickens was wrong.

Very wrong.

Chapter 3

Staplehurst, Kent. 3:05 p.m.

Old John Benge stretched and held his aching back. He pulled out a red handkerchief and mopped the sweat off his brow.

"We're doing well, lads. Just the last two rails to put back on the bridge. Shall we stop for tea? Or finish the job and go home early?"

The men muttered among themselves. Little Tommy stood and stared to the east. Old John Benge shook his head.

"Listen, young Tom, if you are that worried about a train coming, then why don't you be our look-out?"

The boy nodded and grinned.

"You're not much help at lifting these rails. Go half a mile down the track," the foreman said, pointing and speaking slowly so the half-deaf boy could understand. "If you see a train coming from the East then wave this red flag. The driver will know it's a sign to stop." Then he muttered, "But you won't see a train because my timetable says you won't."

Benge handed the boy a soot-stained flag from the tool box. Tommy ran off along the side of the track, happier now.

Old John sighed. He turned to the workmen. "It says here on the railway timetable – no train till four o'clock. And the railway timetable is never wrong. Never."

Tommy reached the top of a small rise. He could see the iron bridge and the rail workers behind him. To the east he could see the summer fields stretching away towards the distant sea.

He shaded his eyes. Nothing but corn and woods, haystacks and barns, clouds that looked like sheep, and sheep that looked like clouds. Even his poor ears could hear the blackbirds singing in the warm afternoon sun. The sky was as blue as a jackdaw's eye.

And there, from behind a clump of trees came a sight that turned the sun on his skin to ice.

A curl of pale smoke rose into the air.

Tommy gasped. He turned to run back towards the bridge to warn the rail gang.

Then his black boots skidded to a halt on the gravel.

"No," he shouted to himself. "Not the bridge. That's too late. I need to warn the *train*."

He threw off his sweaty blue jacket and ran towards the growing plume of smoke, shirt-sleeves flapping and flag held tight. At last the locomotive appeared around the bend.

Tommy stopped. He panted. He planted his feet firmly and raised the red flag.

He could feel the rail by the side of his foot begin to tremble. Even the blackbirds fell silent.

3:08 p.m.

The driver checked the dials on the front of the engine cab. "A bit more coal, Jim. Not too much. It's a downhill run to Staplehurst."

The fireman opened the door to the firebox and the blast of hot air hit him in the face as he placed some

large nuggets of coal carefully on the grate. "Not too much, not too little," he said.

The driver nodded. "The more coal we save, the more money they pay us. Anyway, I was telling you about our famous passenger, Mr Dickens, and his new story. That's all about money too."

"Never mind the money – you should be looking for the signals," the fireman grumbled.

The driver laughed. "All the signals will be set to green today," he said with a shrug. "I've seen the timetable. No trains between twelve o'clock and four o'clock through Kent."

"Except us," Jim said.

"Except us. We are the boat train. We run when the ferry boat from France lands, and that changes every day. It depends on the tides so we aren't on the main timetable.

The signalmen will wave us straight through, though."

"You should still be keeping a lookout," Jim argued. He stepped to the side of the cab and peered out. Something caught his eye. "Here, what was that?"

The driver joined him. "What was what?"

"We've passed him now," Jim shouted, looking back, as the warm wind whistled round their ears. "Look ... behind us. A boy waving a red flag. Nearly missed him."

"Some kid playing a daft game."

"He could be the lookout for a rail gang, we should slow down."

"Did he have a blue uniform on?"

"No, but ..."

"Then he's probably just mucking

about. Let me see," the driver said with a sigh. "What's ahead?"

"Staplehurst Bridge," Jim reminded him.

The driver rubbed his eyes and peered ahead. "Looks like some men working there. We'd better slow down."

"No," Jim shouted. "We need to *stop*."

The driver reached for the brass brake lever and began to tug at it. "A bit late now – we're doing forty-five miles an hour. Oh, dear."

The man jerked at the lever and felt the engine shudder and skid, squeal and scream as it swept on towards Old John Benge and his gang of shocked workmen.

Chapter 4

Staplehurst, Kent. 3:11 p.m.

The wheels on the engine stopped but the eight heavy carriages pushed it on, skidding and sparking.

The guards in the carriages felt the train slow and turned the wheels that would put on the brakes on the carriages.

In the first-class carriage Charles Dickens was sitting with his back to the engine. He felt his head snap back against the seat.

But the two women and Matilda the maid were facing the engine. They were

thrown forward across the carriage like rag dolls.

Ellen Ternan screamed in pain. Her mother struck her head and lay silent. Matilda stretched out an arm and felt a sharp pain in her wrist.

The screech of the wheels stopped as the locomotive ran off the end of the tracks and onto the wood frame of the bridge.

It shuddered and slowed and, for a moment, seemed to have safely stopped. Then there was a splintering, cracking, creaking, groaning as the bridge broke. The engine rolled.

"Jump!" the driver cried to his fireman, Jim. The two men leapt into the stream and waded to the muddy bank. They looked up to see the carriages lean over towards the water below them. The men limped and struggled away from the toppling machine.

The carriages in the middle began to roll – slowly, like a man clinging to a cliff by his finger-tips. For half a second it looked as if they would settle at a drunken angle. Then a beam of wood snapped like a pistol-shot and the carriages moved again. They rolled off the bridge and hit the stream in a cloud of spray.

They split and smashed. A handful of
people were thrown out of the broken
doors onto the bushy banks below.

There was silence. The twisted train lay
still. The locomotive at the front hissed,

people sobbed, and somewhere a bird still sang.

Then Old John Benge's voice cried, "Get these people out," and his men rushed towards the carriages to tear open the doors.

The coaches at the back were still on the track though many of their passengers were bruised and broken. They were led to the edge of the track to sit on the warm grass bank and tend to their cuts from the shattered windows.

Then the workmen headed towards the front of the train where the coaches were hanging over the mangled bridge.

Suddenly a door was kicked open and Charles Dickens leaned out, his head bleeding and his hair wild.

"Get my friends out," he ordered. The men scrambled down into the stream and stretched up their arms as the  writer passed Matilda down. She sobbed softly as her aching wrist was grasped and she was led to safety.

Then the groaning Ellen Ternan

followed. Her mother was slid clumsily after her and her limp body half-fell into the arms of the waiting men. They laid her on the bank of the stream and found water-bottles in their dinner-sacks to pour over her face. "She's alive," a man muttered.

Charles Dickens dropped his case to the river-bank. It burst open and a few papers were caught on the summer breeze and drifted away into the River Beult.

The writer lowered himself down beside Ellen Ternan. "She's alive," he said. "Just a bang to the head. Look after the ones who need help the most. The bleeding. The broken. The dying."

The writer's powerful voice carried over the moans and cries of the injured. "Ellen, look after your mother," he ordered.

"I hurt my leg," she sniffled.

"Then you are one of the lucky ones," he replied. "There are people far worse off than you, my dear."

"Stay and look after me," she whimpered.

"No," he snapped as he walked away. "You will live. There are others who need my help more."

"But Charles!" she cried.

He marched up the side of the stream, half-deaf to her pleading voice.

At that moment the gasping Tommy Bucket ran up to the scene and Charles Dickens gripped him by the arm. "Are you hurt, boy?"

Tommy shook his head.

"Then run into Staplehurst town and fetch as many people as you can. Doctors, carters, workmen ... anyone."

"Y-y-y-" Tommy said.

The writer sighed. "You're dumb, are you, lad?"

"N-n-n-"

"You're no use if you can't explain." Dickens looked around. "Matilda," he called to the maid. "Go to the town. Tell them what happened. The boy will show you the way."

"Yes sir," the maid nodded. She clutched at her wrist, and ran as fast as Tommy towards the distant town.

Dickens looked down on the smoking wreck. "Let's see what we can do, till help gets here," he said.

Chapter 5

Staplehurst, Kent. 5:30 p.m.

Tommy and Matilda returned an hour later with a crowd of helpers, and many more who just wanted to gawp and gawk and stare at the disaster.

They ran over to Charles Dickens, who was covering a man's face with a handkerchief. He looked up at the couple and gave a pained smile.

"You did well," he said. "Now find a doctor and let him look at your wrist, child," he told the maid.

"I need to see to Miss Ternan. She'll be angry. I left her," Matilda mumbled.

Dickens looked down at the man on the ground. "I have seen some pitiful sights here today," he said. "I gave this man with a cracked skull some water, then went to help a lady with a gash on her leg. By the time I came back to the man he was dead. Miss Ternan will be fine. See to yourself, child."

"What can I do?" Tommy Bucket asked.

The writer looked at him sharply. "You can speak?"

"I – I had a bad shock. B-but ... this is so much w-worse," the boy whispered. "It makes my nightmare seem silly and small." He looked up at the haunted eyes of the writer. "So what can I do?"

Dickens looked up at the carriage that hung over the edge of the bridge. "My boy, you have done a lot. These poor passengers have all the help they need. But ... but there is one favour you can do me. Something for which twenty thousand people will thank you."

"What is it?"

"Climb into the carriage there, the one I was riding in, and find my notebook. I had just finished the next chapter of *Our Mutual Friend*. Save it or it will be lost forever."

The writer lifted the boy into the air. He was light as the steam rising from the stream. Tommy crawled through the broken door. He thought he felt the carriage shift. He waited.

The book was just beyond his finger tips. He stretched. His fingers felt the paper and he tugged it towards him.

The movement made him slide backwards. He tumbled through the door into the arms of the writer, and the notebook fell into the stream.

Dickens snatched the book and shook it. He smiled. "Not too much damage, my lad. You are the real hero of this disaster."

Tommy looked around at the scarred riverbank and the broken people being loaded onto carts. An old man staggered towards them. His eyes were empty as the sky and his mouth hung open. It was Old John Benge.

He muttered over and over, "The railway timetable is never wrong. Never. Never wrong. Never."

"I tried to tell him," Tommy sighed.

"And I tried to tell Matilda this train wouldn't stop before it reached London," Charles Dickens said. "The old are not always right."

Five years later.

Higham, Kent, 9 June 1865 3:11 p.m.

Tommy knocked on the kitchen door to the mansion at Gad's Hill. It was five years after the Staplehurst crash and he now held the job that Old John Benge once had, as leader of the repair gang. Old John had been as broken as the carriages after the crash and never worked again.

Now Tommy was dressed in his black Sunday suit and his best boots shone like mirrors. Matilda opened the door and smiled at him – a welcoming but weak smile. She was chief housemaid in Mr Dickens' house.

"Come in, Tommy," she said quietly. "I knew you'd come. You always visit on this day, the ninth of June."

"And you're always pleased to see me," he said. "But not today. What have I done?"

Matilda took a kettle from the kitchen stove and poured boiling water into a teapot.

"You've done nothing, Tommy. It's Mr Dickens."

"I saw the coaches outside the front door – he has so many visitors. Who are they? What's happening?"

Matilda stirred the tea and placed it on the table while she took some blue and white cups and saucers from the cupboard. "They are Mr Dickens' children," she explained. "Mr Henry Dickens said he'd let me know what happens upstairs."

"They've come to remember this day five years ago, the same as me?" he asked.

"No," she said slowly as she poured the tea and added milk. "After the crash, Mr Dickens was afraid of trains. Before the disaster he thought they were the greatest thing ever. But after the accident he would often get off a train early and walk the rest of the way.

"He found writing much harder. It wore him out. It made him ill."

"But he's still not an old man," Tommy argued. "He'll get better if he rests."

"He was never strong before the crash. He started to have terrors in the night. Panics when he travelled – even in a horse-drawn cab. I have been with him on a slow train when it gave a rattle and he started to sweat and shiver."

Tommy nodded slowly. "I know how he feels. I couldn't speak after my accident.

But I was young. I got over it."

Matilda looked at him carefully. "Mr Dickens fell really ill last week. They do not think he will get over it."

At that moment the door to the kitchen opened. A man with dark side-whiskers stood there and looked wearily at Matilda. "Tea for the family, please, Matilda."

"Yes, Mr Henry. How is Mr Dickens?" she asked.

Charles Dickens' son shook his head. "It's over," he replied and closed the door softly.

Matilda looked at the shocked face of Tommy as his tea grew cold in his hand. "Five years ago on this very day, the Staplehurst crash killed ten people. Today it killed number eleven," she said.

True History

The Staplehurst rail crash was a railway accident in Kent, England. Ten passengers died and forty more were injured.

The railway line was being repaired at a spot where it ran over a low bridge crossing the River Beult. The foreman thought that the next train would arrive much later, and the last two rails had not been laid. His timetable SAID there would be no train. He was looking at the wrong timetable.

The Folkestone Boat Express was due to set off when a passenger ship arrived from France. The ship set off when the tide was high... that tide changed every day of course. So the Boat Express timetable changed every day, too. The foreman checked the Boat Express timetable – but he looked at the page for the day before. He thought the Boat Express wouldn't come through until 5.20 that afternoon, long after their work was done. In fact it came nearly two hours earlier.

The foreman had a lookout, but he couldn't give enough warning of the fast approaching train – he wasn't far enough away. The engine managed to reach the far side of the bridge but the wooden bridge cracked, and most of the carriages fell into the shallow River Beult.

The accident is famous because the writer Charles Dickens was on board with his girlfriend, Nell Ternan. He helped many of the injured and saw some of them die.

The crash bothered him for the rest of his life. It made him ill and afraid of trains. The accident happened in 1865 on 9 June. Charles Dickens died five years later in 1870... on 9 June.

Did the shock of the crash shorten his life?

You try

1. Charles Dickens was a great writer and lots of people like to meet their favourite authors. If you could meet your favourite author (alive or dead) what FIVE questions would you ask them?

2. Charles Dickens wrote a letter to a friend after the accident. The letter began ...

'I was in the only carriage that did not go over into the stream.'

It ended...

'But in writing these words, and remembering the accident, I feel the shake and am forced to stop.
Yours faithfully,
Charles Dickens'

Can you fill in the letter between that start and the end?

3. Imagine you are the Prime Minister of Britain at the time of the accident. (He was called Viscount Palmerston, by the way.)

What FIVE new laws would YOU invent to make sure an accident like Staplehurst never happened again?

Tudor Tales

Exciting, funny stories based on real events...
welcome to the Tudor times!

Terry Deary's Shakespeare Tales

If you liked this book
why not look out for the rest of
Terry Deary's Shakespeare Tales?
Meet Shakespeare and his
theatre company!

World War II Tales

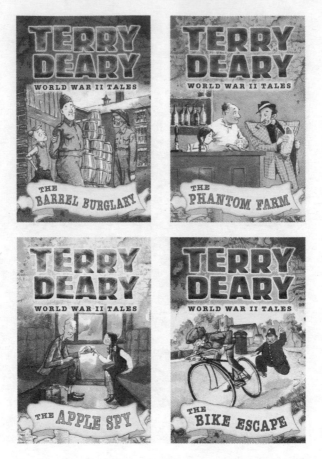

Exciting, funny stories based on real events...
welcome to World War II!